Hi, Earthlings, my name is Zip.
Come visit me on Planet Blip.

We'll zoom around in my spaceship.

You'll see cool sights on our little trip!

We'll drop by to visit my buddy Kip...

and have a moonball championship.

The loser buys ice cream—quadruple dip!
(Just be careful not to drip!)

You'll meet my pet. He's called a pip.

Instead of barking, he says, "Mip! Mip!"
Instead of running, he likes to skip.

When we curl his hair, he looks really hip.

We'll hike 'round a crater—
be careful, don't slip!

We'll jump in the middle to take a dip…

then watch the comets whirl and whip.

Oh, please do visit Planet Blip.
You'll love it here. You'll really flip!

Listen to the riddle sentences. Add the right letter or letters to the -ip sound to finish each one.

**1** During summer vacation my family and I will go on a ___ip.

**2** Don't step on the banana peel or else you might Sl___ip!

**3** We eat our ice cream cones fast so that they don't ___ip.

**4** She held her hair back with a hair ___ip.

**5** I poured a glass of milk and took a big ___ip.

**6** On Halloween, I put a fake mustache above my __ip.

**7** My chocolate chip cookie only had one ___ip!

**8** In gymnastics, I learned to do a back ___ip.

**9** My dad calls two scoops of ice cream a double __ip.

**10** Below your waist is your __ip.

Now make up some new riddle sentences using -ip

**Answers:** 1. trip, 2. slip, 3. drip, 4. clip, 5. sip, 6. lip, 7. chip, 8. flip, 9. dip, 10. hip.

# -ip Cheer

Give a great holler, a cheer, a yell

For all of the words that we can spell

With an I and a P that make the sound –ip,

You'll find it in sip and hip and trip.

Two little letters, that's all that we need

To make a whole family of words to read!

Make a list of other –ip words. Then use them in the cheer!